BAD BOYZ:
K.O. KINGS

ALAN DURANT

WALKER BOOKS
AND SUBSIDIARIES

LONDON · BOSTON · SYDNEY · AUCKLAND

First published 2002 by Walker Books Ltd
87 Vauxhall Walk, London SE11 5HJ

4 6 8 10 9 7 5

Text © 2002 Alan Durant
Bad Boyz logo © 2001 Phil Schramm
Cover photography by Cliff Birtchell
Cover design by Walker Books Ltd

This book has been typeset in Futura book

Printed and bound in Great Britain by
J. H. Haynes & Co. Ltd. Sparkford

British Library Cataloguing in Publication Data:
a catalogue record for this book is
available from the British Library

ISBN 0-7445-5991-X

BAD BOYZ: K.O. KINGS

Alan Durant has been football mad since he was eight. On the field, he peaked early, playing for two seasons in the Collingwood Boys Junior School football team, scoring one goal! After that, it was all downhill. He supports Manchester United and his favourite player of all time is George Best, after whom he named his one and only goldfish. Sadly, the goldfish died. He has passed his football talents on to his son Kit, who plays in a little league – and around the house with a pair of rolled-up socks. Bad Boyz is based on children Alan has met during his career as an author and football spectator ... you know who you are!

Alan Durant's football stories have appeared in various anthologies, including two collections of *Gary Lineker's Favourite Football Stories*; *On Me 'Ead, Santa*; and *Football Shorts*. He is also the author of the Leggs United series about a family football team managed by a ghost. The series and Alan himself were featured in a recent Children's Bafta Award-winning programme on BBC TV. His other work ranges from picture books for young children to novels and mystery stories for young adults. Alan lives just south of London with his wife, Jinny, and three children, Amy, Kit and Josie. He doesn't expect to get a call from Sven Goran Eriksson.

04912

Books by the same author

Bad Boyz: Kicking Off
Leagues Apart
Barmy Army

Creepe Hall
Return to Creepe Hall
Creepe Hall For Ever!
Jake's Magic
Star Quest: Voyage to the Greylon Galaxy
Spider McDrew
Happy Birthday, Spider McDrew
Little Troll
Little Troll and the Big Present
Leggs United (series)
Football Fun

This book is dedicated with thanks to Vauxhall Primary School in London and all the children who posed for the Bad Boyz covers.

1

"Catch it, Kyle, you big blob!"

The Bad Boyz keeper turned and glared at the shouting figure on the touch-line. He'd just palmed a fierce shot round the post and he reckoned it had been a pretty good save.

"Don't take any notice," said Jordan. She clapped a hand on Kyle's broad shoulder. "That was wicked."

"Who *is* that geezer, anyway?" growled Sadiq, waving a clenched fist towards the touch-line.

"Yeah, who's he calling a big blob?" said Max. "Great ugly gorilla." He put his hands in his armpits, pulled a face and started making gorilla noises. Next to him, Bloomer squeaked with laughter and joined in. They were still monkeying around when the corner came over. Luckily, Dareth, the captain, was paying attention to the game and booted the ball clear.

"Come on, Bad Boyz! Concentrate!" called Mr Davies. He was both the Bad Boyz manager and a teacher at their school. He glanced along the touch-line. He was used to being his team's only supporter and he wondered who the man was who'd shouted at Kyle.

Mr Davies had never seen him before, but he was obviously someone who knew Kyle well. All his comments had been directed at the keeper – and none had been complimentary. Fortunately, Kyle was in a pretty good mood. The match was almost over and he hadn't let in a goal. At the other end, Bad Boyz had struck three times and were well set for a comfortable win.

It was the first round of the Appleton Little League Cup. Bad Boyz' opponents were X Club 7. In his pre-match team talk, Mr Davies had called them "the most improved team in the league".

"Yeah," Dareth had agreed. "But they're still pants."

They'd looked anything but pants in the first half, though. The game had been very even and Kyle had had to make a number of fine saves – though none of them good enough for the man on the touch-line, it seemed. When Kyle parried the ball, he should have caught it; when he saved with his feet, he should have used his hands; when he booted the ball clear, he should have picked it up...

By half-time, only one goal had separated the teams – and that had been a fluke. A corner from Jordan had rebounded off the post, hit a defender on the heel and bounced back over the line.

In the second half, though, Bad Boyz had been well on top. Sung-Woo, their main striker, had scored twice and could have got three or four more. Jordan had hit the post with a scorching shot and Dareth had had a header cleared off the line.

To their credit, X Club 7 carried on battling to the end, even though they were obviously very tired. It was due to this tiredness that they gave away a penalty in the last minute. A weary defender stumbled and tripped Sung-Woo as the striker chased a long kick from

Kyle. It was a clear penalty.

Dareth offered the ball to Sung-Woo. "You take it," he said. "Get your hat-trick."

But Sung-Woo shook his head with a characteristic frown. "You the penalty taker," he insisted. "I have two goals already. You score."

Dareth shrugged. "All right. Cheers!" he said.

He placed the ball on the spot and took a couple of steps backwards. Then he trotted forward and blasted it into the top right-hand corner of the net. At once he wheeled round and began his latest celebration. This involved cupping one hand round his ear and flapping the other like a wing. He was well into this before he noticed that no one else was joining in. They were all just standing looking at him.

Dareth's hands dropped and so did his smile. "Wassup?" he said, puzzled.

Jordan nodded towards the goal. "Look," she said.

Dareth turned. The referee was still standing by the penalty spot with his arms folded. "Take it again," he ordered. "And this time, wait till I blow my whistle."

10

"I thought you did blow," said Dareth.

The referee shook his head.

Dareth grinned. "Must have been Bloomer, then," he said.

Once more he placed the ball on the penalty spot.

Once more he took a couple of steps back.

He waited.

The referee blew his whistle.

Once more, Dareth ran forward and blasted the ball ... but this time into the top left-hand corner.

He raised his hands and started to turn, but before he could, Bloomer and Max had jumped him. A moment later, Kyle tumbled on top and all four fell in a screeching heap.

The mystery man on the touch-line was not amused. "Get back in goal, Kyle, you idiot!" he barked. "The game's not over!" But he was wrong. For at that instant the referee blew the final whistle.

Bad Boyz had beaten X Club 7 by 4–0 – the same score as in the league. They were through to the next round of the cup.

2

"Who was that bloke?" asked Jordan when Bad Boyz were back in the changing-room.

"What a pain in the butt," said Max. "Kyle, get back in goal," he mimicked in a ridiculous husky voice, "pick the ball up, catch that cross, stop scratching your nuts."

"Yeah, what was his problem anyway?" Sadiq added.

"Is he a relative or sumfing?" Dareth asked.

Kyle's small eyes narrowed to tiny dots. "Yeah," he huffed. "He's me dad, ain't 'e."

The others all stared at Kyle. But no one said anything. They'd heard about Kyle's dad.

"I thought he was in prison," Dareth muttered finally.

"They let him out, didn't they," said Kyle resentfully. "Now he's come back round here to cause trouble."

"Can't your mum do anything about it?" Jordan suggested.

Kyle shook his large head with resignation. "She can't do nuffing. She's scared of him, ain't she. Everyone is."

"I'm not," said Sadiq defiantly.

"Yeah, well, that's cos you're a wally," said Kyle. "My dad 'ud rip yer 'ead off." He punched his goalie top into his kit-bag.

The door opened and Mr Davies came in.

"Well played, everyone," he said. His cheeriness died away at the sight of the gloomy faces before him. "What's up?" he asked.

"It's him out there," said Jordan.

"Yeah, who is he?" Mr Davies enquired. "It's the first time I've seen him round here."

"He's Kyle's dad," said Jordan.

"They let him out of prison," said Max.

"'e's 'ard," piped Bloomer.

"Well, he was certainly hard on you, Kyle," said Mr Davies consolingly. "I thought you had a brilliant match."

"He don't think I'm no good at nuffing," Kyle grumbled. "He never has. Not that he can talk.

The only fing he's any good at is makin' trouble."

"Well, maybe you should stay away from him," said Mr Davies. "Unless you *want* to see him, of course," he continued quickly. "He is your dad after all."

"I don't want to have nuffing to do with him," Kyle huffed. He tugged the zip on his bag and walked towards the door. "I hate his guts."

Mr Davies looked after his keeper anxiously. Trouble was never far away from Bad Boyz and he had a feeling it was about to pay them another visit.

3

Monday was cold and grey. A chilly wind huffed about the school playground like an irritable two-year-old. So did Kyle. He got in a fight and ended up in detention. For once, he was all alone.

The seven members of the Bad Boyz team were no strangers to detention. They had spent many, many lunchtimes twiddling their thumbs in a classroom while the rest of the school could be heard laughing and playing outside. It was to keep them out of detention that Mr Davies had proposed forming a seven-a-side football team.

For the most part, the scheme had been a success. Bad Boyz were no angels, but they weren't half as much trouble as they had been. Even the dour head-teacher Mr Fisher (alias Piranha) was impressed by their "improvement". Sadiq was less difficult and more polite, he noted. Bloomer didn't talk so much in class and was concentrating better. Jordan had curbed her graffiti habit and improved her communication skills. Max didn't play the fool quite so often. Sung-Woo's English had come on hugely and he actually did his homework. Dareth had apparently abandoned the criminal activities for which he was infamous. And Kyle had learnt to control his temper and not get into fights.

Until now.

"What happened, Kyle?" Mr Davies enquired. "And don't say you 'didn't do nuffing'." "I didn't do nuffing" was Kyle's catchphrase.

"I didn't," Kyle grumbled. "Well, not much. I was just helpin' out Jordan."

Mr Davies smiled. If there was one person who didn't need helping out, it was Jordan. She may be the only girl in the Bad Boyz team, but she could more than hold her own. She wasn't a girl to be messed with.

"Just don't get involved, Kyle, OK?" Mr Davies instructed.

Kyle humphed. Something was obviously upsetting him – and being given a detention, Mr Davies was sure, wasn't it.

"Is it your dad that's worrying you?" he probed.

"Huh, him," Kyle humphed.

"Is he going to stay around for long?"

"Long enough to make my life a misery. He always does. He gets out of prison, comes back and causes trouble. Then he goes off again."

"Where?"

"Back inside, usually."

"Well, try not to let him get to you too much. I mean, like you say, he'll be gone again soon."

"Yeah, I s'pose."

"And you've got a semi-final to look forward to."

There were only eight teams in the Appleton Little League, so winning one match put you into the semi-final.

"I hope he don't come to watch," Kyle said gloomily. "I hate him being there."

At that moment, the door swung open and Bloomer's pink face appeared.

"Sir! Someone's thrown up in the toilets!" he squeaked. "There's bits of carrot and tomato and peas and stuff all over the floor. And there's this big pool of—"

"Yes, thanks, Bloomer. I get the picture." Mr Davies sighed. "I'll come and sort it out..."

4

At the next training session, Mr Davies introduced a new crossing exercise. The team's shooting had improved a lot, he said, but they needed to create more goal chances.

The idea was simple enough: one player crossed the ball from the wing, another ran in to the centre of the goal, and, when the ball came over, tried to score. The reality, however, was not so straightforward.

After twenty minutes, not a single goal had been scored. Only two crosses had found their target – and these had been easily saved by Kyle, even though he wasn't allowed to move out of his goal.

Some crosses went behind their intended target; some went over the waiting player's head; some rolled straight into Kyle's hands.

One, by Sadiq, was so badly sliced that it flew away in the opposite direction and hit the roof of the caretaker's hut.

Finally, a left-footed cross by Bloomer was flicked into the net by Sung-Woo. The striker, as usual, was unmoved, but Bloomer jumped about as if he'd just scored the winning goal in a cup final.

"Well done, Bloomer. But that's how you should be crossing the ball every time," Mr Davies chided. "One out of five isn't good enough."

"It's better than nought out of five," Jordan remarked drily. "Like Bloomer usually gets in his maths tests."

Bloomer blushed. "No I never!" he squawked indignantly. "I got nought outta *ten* last week." The others laughed.

"Well, anyway," Mr Davies reiterated, "you've got to get those crosses more accurate. We'll carry on with the exercise at our next session. And to make it more difficult, I'm going to let Kyle come off his line."

"Oh no, then we'll *never* score," Dareth moaned.

"Course we will!" said Sadiq confidently.

"By the time old slow-mo gets near the cross, the ball'll already be in the goal." It was the kind of comment that was usually guaranteed to bring a heated response from Kyle. That's why Sadiq had made it. But today, Kyle didn't even shrug. His mind was evidently on other things. And they all knew what.

"I've got some news for you," Mr Davies announced. "The draw's been made for the semi-final. The good news is, we're not playing Terminators." Terminators were the team that had finished third in the league. "The bad news is that we're playing Hornets." There was a collective groan. Hornets had finished second in the league behind Bad Boyz, and they were the only team to have beaten them so far. "The other semi-final's between Terminators and Eddy's Eagles." Eddy's Eagles were one of the weaker teams in the Appleton Little League.

"Why couldn't we have drawn Eagles?" Bloomer moaned.

"Yeah, we'd've beaten them easy," said Sadiq.

Only Dareth seemed happy – relieved almost – with the draw. "We'd have to 'ave played Hornets sometime," he said, "so it may as well be now. Besides, Eddy's Eagles have got some new players. They're stronger than they was."

"I'd still rather play them than the Hornets," Sadiq insisted.

"Dareth's right," Mr Davies said cheerily. "Think of it as a challenge. It's about time we beat the Hornets." As well as the league match, Bad Boyz had played Hornets in a trial game before the season started. That match had been a 3–3 draw. "You've improved a lot since you last played them."

Bloomer thrust his hand in the air. "Sir, sir! Do you think *I've* improved?" he squealed.

"Yes, I do, Bloomer," Mr Davies laughed. "I think you all have."

Bloomer's cheeks were pink with pleasure.

"You're still a dir, though," Jordan remarked.

5

The first half of the game against Hornets went like a dream.

For a start, there was no sign of Kyle's dad, which gave Kyle a real boost. He smiled for the first time in about a week.

The weather seemed to be in tune with his mood. It had been gloomy and overcast all week, but on Saturday morning the sun shone. And in their bright yellow shirts, Bad Boyz dazzled. The training sessions appeared to have had a very positive effect on their passing and movement, which was much sharper than it had been in the game against X Club 7. And it needed to be, for Hornets were a much better side. They didn't have any outstanding individuals, but they played well together and were very difficult to break down.

On this particular day, however, Dareth was on top form. He was full of tricks — dummies, step-overs, nutmegs, flicks and backheels… He tried them all, and, for the most part, they came off. Every time he got the ball, he looked dangerous. He set up the opening goal with a mazy run through the Hornets' midfield, followed by a clever reverse pass to Jordan, who rammed the ball into the net. The Hornets keeper didn't even move.

The second goal was even better. Bloomer ran with the ball from just outside the Bad Boyz penalty area to the halfway line, before passing inside to Dareth. Instead of trapping the ball, Dareth let it run between his legs, spinning quickly to leave the nearest Hornets player beaten completely. A neat step-over, and the Bad Boyz skipper was past a second Hornets player. A dodge and a dart took him beyond two more with only the keeper to beat. There was no way he was going to miss. As the keeper stepped forward, Dareth rifled the ball into the bottom left-hand corner of the net.

An instant later he was standing by the touch-line with one hand cupped round an ear and the other waving by his waist.

An instant more and Max and Bloomer had joined him, copying his actions.

Mr Davies shook his head and smiled.

By half-time, the score was 3–0. And in many ways, to the manager at least, the third goal was the most satisfying. For it was a goal straight from the training ground. A clearance by Sadiq found Jordan on the halfway line. She controlled the ball and fed it through to Sung-Woo. He took the ball with his back to the goal, kept it briefly and then played it out to the right wing into the space towards which Jordan was now sprinting. She got to the ball just before a Hornets defender, knocked it beyond him and crossed the ball on the run. The ball and Sung-Woo arrived in the centre of the goal at the same moment and, without breaking stride, the striker clipped a clean half-volley into the top of the net. It was breathtaking stuff and drew spontaneous applause from all round the pitch. Bad Boyz were 3–0 up and looking irresistible.

Hornets weren't playing badly, but they couldn't cope with the speed, invention and skill of the Bad Boyz attacking play, while at the other end of the pitch Kyle was superb.

Cheered by his dad's absence, he was having the match of his life. Whatever the Hornets threw at him, he caught. No matter how fierce the shot, he held it. He looked unbeatable.

At 3–0, with half the match gone and his team playing brilliantly, Mr Davies could have been excused for thinking that a place in the final was as good as won. But with Bad Boyz, nothing was ever that certain. Besides, as everyone knows, football is a game of two halves…

6

The trouble began right at the start of the second half when Kyle's dad appeared. Within moments of the kick-off, he'd started shouting. The effect on Kyle was extraordinary. His confidence waned visibly. He fumbled the first shot he had to save, and Max had to boot the ball clear for a corner.

"Get a grip, Butterfingers!" Kyle's dad sneered.

"Just ignore him," Jordan encouraged her keeper. But Kyle couldn't. He missed the ball completely when it came over from the corner. Luckily, Dareth was behind him and headed it away.

But the next time the ball came Kyle's way, there was no one on hand to rescue him. Bad Boyz had managed to keep Hornets at bay for several minutes, protecting their vulnerable keeper, and it looked as though they'd done so again when Max cleared a corner to the halfway line. The ball fell to a Hornets defender, who took a few steps forward before hoofing it high into the air towards the Bad Boyz goal. The ball went over the heads of attackers and defenders alike and dropped straight into Kyle's hands. Unfortunately, it dropped straight out again and landed at the feet of a waiting Hornets attacker, who had the simple task of side-footing the ball into the net.

Now Kyle's dad really gave him some stick. "Call yourself a goalie!" he jeered. "You couldn't catch a cold!"

Mr Davies tried to sound a more positive note. "Come on, Kyle!" he urged. "Keep your head up."

For Kyle, though, the dream had turned into a nightmare. His dad's constant taunts and criticisms reduced him to a blundering wreck. His handling was terrible. He just couldn't hold onto anything. It was as if his gloves were coated with grease.

Bad Boyz had put a lot of effort into the first

half and it told on them as the second half went by. Sung-Woo became increasingly isolated up front, as none of the midfield players had the energy to link up with him. Even so, he very nearly settled the game, midway though the second half, with a speculative, long-range shot that beat the Hornets goalie but bounced against the frame of the goal.

For the final ten minutes, Bad Boyz defended desperately – and with a large slice of luck. Somehow, each time Kyle dropped the ball it fell to one of his own players or went past the post. Twice Hornets hit the bar.

With just minutes left, Hornets mounted another attack. Once again, the ball was pumped into the Bad Boyz penalty area. Wearily, Max swung a foot to clear the danger – but missed his kick entirely. The ball ran through to a Hornets player.

"Move yourself, Kyle, you great lump!" shouted Kyle's dad as the Hornets player advanced on goal. But Kyle seemed to be frozen to his line. The Hornets player had almost the whole goal to aim at. All he had to do was kick the ball to either side of Kyle to score. But he didn't. He shot straight at the keeper and without any power. It was more like a pass than a shot. Normally, Kyle would have saved it easily. Normally. Today, in his jittery state, he let the ball roll between his legs. He turned to grab it, but the ball had already crossed the line. The Hornets had pulled another goal back and Kyle dropped to the ground in despair.

"Dodgy keeper, dodgy keeper!" Kyle's dad chanted unkindly.

Jordan had had enough. "Why don't you shut up!" she shouted.

"Yeah, leave him alone!" Sadiq added hotly.

Kyle's dad laughed unpleasantly. He made a rude gesture with his finger.

"Hey!" Mr Davies shouted. He walked towards Kyle's dad, and the referee and the manager of the Hornets did the same. A heated exchange followed, at the end of which Kyle's dad walked away.

"I'll be back," he called menacingly, and he made another rude gesture before departing.

There were still a few minutes of the match left, but the break seemed to have affected everyone. Hornets didn't look like they would be adding to their two goals and Bad Boyz were happy to play out time.

When the referee blew his whistle for the end of the game there were no great celebrations by the winners. They shook hands with their opponents and offered three cheers. Hornets did the same. Then they all headed wearily for the changing-rooms.

7

For a team that was about to play in a cup final, Bad Boyz were oddly subdued, Mr Davies thought as he watched them at the end of their training session that Thursday. The shadow of Kyle's dad seemed to loom large over all of them – not just Kyle. Even the news that their opponents in the final were not to be Terminators, as had been expected, but Eddy's Eagles, barely lifted their spirits. Indeed, in Dareth's case it had exactly the opposite effect. He met the news as if he'd just been told he had to eat nothing but cabbage for rest of the week.

"I thought you'd be pleased, Dareth," Mr Davies said.

"Yeah, I am," said the Bad Boyz skipper. "It's great."

Then why has your face gone so pale? thought his coach. But he didn't get the chance to pose the question, because Dareth was already on his way back inside.

Mr Davies did have a word with Kyle, though. The big goalkeeper had been in a quiet, glum mood all week. In the school staffroom, some of the teachers had taken to calling him The Incredible Sulk. To Mr Davies, however, Kyle's mood was anything but a joke. If he performed in the final like he had in the second half of the semi-final, then Bad Boyz would be in deep trouble. Besides, his gloominess was affecting the whole team.

"Have you talked to your mum about what's happening – you know, with your dad?" Mr Davies asked.

"No," Kyle grunted. "She wouldn't be able to do nuffing anyway."

"Does he come round to the house?"

"No. He ain't allowed, is he. There's a court order. He has to stay away." His podgy face glooped into a scowl. "He used to come back and beat her up, didn't he. He can't do that no more."

"In that case, he's probably not allowed to

33

bother you either," said Mr Davies. "This sounds like a police matter."

"No, it ain't. We don't want nuffing to do with the police." His face was red with vexation. Mr Davies didn't press the matter. He suspected there were things that went on in Kyle's family – as in the families of many of the children at the school – that they wouldn't want the police to know about. In a tough area like theirs, it was a fact of life.

"But you need to face this thing, Kyle," said Mr Davies. "Either you have it out with your dad, or you've got to try to ignore him. Otherwise you're going to let yourself – and the rest of the team – down."

"Yeah, I know," Kyle mumbled. His fierce scowl crumpled into an unhappy frown.

"Look, didn't you say that the only thing he's good at is causing trouble?" Mr Davies continued. "Well, don't let him."

"How can I *stop* him?"

"By showing him that you *are* good at something – something worth being good at. You're a bloody good goalie – excuse my language. And you're a vital part of a very good team."

"D'you think so?" Kyle said. The frown lifted a little.

"Of course I do. And so do the others. You were brilliant in the first half against Hornets. Barthez couldn't have been better. Dareth may have created the goals for us, but you stopped Hornets scoring – and that was every bit as important. Play like that in the final and we'll win. Then it won't matter what your dad says. You can wave that trophy in his face and say, 'Look, I've achieved something. I'm a winner'."

Kyle looked doubtful. "Yeah, but what if we lose?"

"Win or lose, as long as you've done your best, you can hold your head up high. We'll all be proud of you."

Kyle sighed. "Yeah," he said. "I'll try to ignore him. I'll do me best." But he didn't sound as positive as Mr Davies had hoped.

Later on that day, Mr Davies asked Dareth if he had any suggestions for raising Kyle's spirits. Dareth was usually good at that sort of thing. But today he just shrugged and said he couldn't think of anything. His mind was obviously on other things.

So Mr Davies turned to Jordan. He was relieved to discover that she was a lot more helpful. She'd speak to the others, she said, and try to come up with something.

She was as good as her word.

The following day, at lunch break, she presented Kyle with a piece of paper rolled up like a scroll. The other Bad Boyz were with her.

"What's this?" Kyle asked suspiciously.

"Unroll it and see," said Jordan.

"We made it for you," said Bloomer proudly.

Kyle unrolled the paper to reveal a home-made certificate.

On the back of the certificate there was a picture of Kyle with a ball in his hands, standing over a dazed eagle.

"Me and Max done most of the writing," said Bloomer excitedly. "Jordan done the picture."

"We did it on the computer," said Max. "Sung-Woo helped us."

"It's good, innit?" piped Bloomer.

"Yeah, it's wicked," Kyle muttered happily. He was clearly very touched by the certificate.

Bad Boyz

Certificate of Xellence

This is to certify that
Kyle Biggins
is the best goalie in Appleton Little League
and also in the world
and also in the univers.

He is also a good geezer even though he never does nuffing!

We also certify that his dad is a right wally and
should go away and stop cawsin truble.

Up the Bad Boyz!

Down the Eagles!

We're gonna win the cup!!!
WAZZA!!!!!

Signed: Jordan Max Sadiq
Bloomer Dareth Sung-Woo

"Fanks," said Kyle. "I'll put it on me wall. I gotta big crack it can cover up."

"You'd need a massive tent to cover up your big crack, man," Sadiq remarked. He nodded at Kyle's large backside. Bloomer and Max laughed.

Sung-Woo looked confused. "You put a tent on your wall?" he asked.

"No, on his butt," said Max. "To cover his butt crack." He bent over and pointed at his own bottom.

Sung-Woo frowned harder than ever. There were times when he simply didn't understand his team-mates at all.

8

There was definitely something up with Dareth. He wasn't his usual chirpy self at all.

Half an hour before the final, Mr Davies saw him behind the changing-rooms talking with two of the players from Eddy's Eagles. It was an animated discussion with a good deal of pointing and finger-waving – mainly by the Eagles players.

When Mr Davies asked Dareth about it later, the Bad Boyz skipper looked sort of shifty.

"It weren't nuffing," he said with a shrug. "I just know 'em, that's all. Their dad used to be me mum's boyfriend." Dareth's mum had had a lot of boyfriends. She was with her latest one now – although just where, no one knew. Dareth was living with his gran until she came back. "He's got a grocer's shop at the end of our road," Dareth added. It seemed to the coach that Dareth was uneasy about something. But what? Was he just nervous about the match?

"That must have been handy," said Mr Davies cheerily, trying to put Dareth at ease.

"Nah, he's a right tight-arse," said Dareth. "He never even gave us a packet of crisps."

Mr Davies nodded. It was time, he decided, to lighten the mood.

"Talking of food," he said loudly to get everyone's attention, "look what I've got for half-time. Not oranges, but—" He pulled a long, thinnish box out of his bag. "Jaffa Cakes!"

"Yeah!" Everyone shouted their approval – even Sung-Woo.

"I thought you'd be pleased," said Mr Davies. "Now, let's get outside and prepare for this game."

Bad Boyz had beaten Eddy's Eagles in the league. The final score had been 5–3 but Bad Boyz should have won much more convincingly. Since the league match, Eagles had added two new players to their squad –

the two boys Dareth had been talking with. According to him they were both good players. In fact, the way he talked about the Eagles, you'd have thought *they* were the favourites, not Bad Boyz.

"Well, we're going to have to be at our best then," said Mr Davies.

Bad Boyz went through their usual warm-up routine of running, jumping and stretching. Then they practised their shooting. While they were doing this, Mr Davies looked around the pitch.

He was disappointed not to see more supporters for his team. He didn't expect much support on a normal Saturday, but today was the Cup Final. He thought that today, at least, more parents might have showed up. Max's dad was there – his milk float was parked by the changing-rooms, so he'd obviously come straight from doing his round. Jordan's dad was there too, which was a pleasant surprise. Jordan had often complained to Mr Davies that her dad never took any interest in her football career. Indeed, Mr Davies had had quite a job convincing him that Jordan should be allowed to play at all. This was the first time her dad had attended a match.

Mr Davies was also pleased that his friend, the Hornets manager, had come to the game to cheer on Bad Boyz. He was standing with the groundsman, Reg Gutteridge, and the secretary of the Appleton Little League, Stan Reynolds.

There was just one other Bad Boyz supporter, and *his* presence wasn't welcomed by anyone. It was Kyle's dad. Mr Davies's pep talk and, especially, the certificate, had boosted Kyle's morale enormously. Now it was about to be put to the test. Would Kyle be able to shut out his dad's barracking and play as everyone knew he could? They'd just have to hope for the best.

At the semi-final, the Hornets manager had reported Kyle's dad's behaviour to the league's ruling committee. Before the game started, Stan Reynolds walked over to Kyle's dad to have a word. He drew his attention to the Little League's guidelines on the attitude of players and spectators. "'Playing for pleasure is more important than winning at all costs'," he quoted from the league manual. "'Emphasis is placed on enjoyment, team spirit and sportsmanship. Parents are asked to encourage players when they do well rather than shouting at them when they make mistakes'."

Kyle's dad wasn't impressed. "Look, mate, he's my son," he said. "I can say what I like to him – and you can't stop me."

"I'm sorry you take that attitude," said the secretary. "But you're wrong. If you break our rules, we are entitled to ask you to leave."

"Yeah? And who's gonna make me – you?" Kyle's dad sneered unpleasantly. He was about a foot taller than the league secretary and about twice as wide.

"Well, let's not let it get to that," Stan Reynolds commented coolly as he walked away.

9

If Kyle's dad was a cause of concern to Mr Davies, the mood of Dareth was equally worrying. The Bad Boyz skipper had none of his customary swagger. Usually he was the life and soul of the team – that's why they'd all chosen him to be captain. But today he looked as if he wished he were somewhere else.

When the referee blew his whistle to summon the two captains, Dareth trudged forward. You'd have thought he was being called for a detention, not a toss-up. Maybe he *was* suffering from nerves, Mr Davies thought – it was the Cup Final, after all. He'd be fine once the match kicked off.

But he wasn't. He started badly and got worse.

His first touch of the ball was to take the

kick-off. He kicked the ball straight to the opposition. They were so surprised that they didn't take advantage and Sung-Woo quickly won the ball back. He passed to Jordan, who ran with the ball almost to the Eagles penalty area. Then just as a defender came to tackle her, she slid the ball cleverly across to Sung-Woo again. He dummied the one defender between him and the goal and thumped the ball into the net. It was 1–0 to Bad Boyz in the very first minute!

Everyone jumped about – except Dareth, who didn't seem happy at all. He cast a nervous glance towards the boys he knew on the Eagles team. One of them pointed a finger at him and scowled.

It was a hard-fought match. Eddy's Eagles had improved and Bad Boyz weren't able to reproduce the sparkling form they'd shown against Hornets. But then Dareth had been their star outfield player that day, and today he was having a nightmare. He gave the ball away so many times in the first half, he might as well have been playing for the Eagles.

Three times Dareth shot wide when he should have scored. On another couple of occasions he failed to pass to Sung-Woo when the striker was totally unmarked in front of goal. His passing was equally bad at the other end of the pitch. Twice his wayward back passes put the Eagles through. Luckily for Bad Boyz, Kyle was playing well. His dad's presence didn't seem to be affecting him, which, in turn, meant there wasn't much for his dad to make remarks about.

There was nothing Kyle could do about the Eagles equalizer, though. It arrived just before half-time and was all down to Dareth. An Eagles corner was headed away by Max, but only to the edge of the penalty area, where it fell to an Eagles player. He hit a fierce shot that Kyle did well to block. The ball dropped to the feet of Dareth, standing on the goal line.

"Clear it!" cried Sadiq.

But Dareth didn't. He just stood staring at the ball, as if it was a bomb or something. His team-mates looked on in horror as the nearest Eagles player stepped forward and tapped the ball over the line into the empty goal.

"What you doin', Dareth?" squeaked Bloomer. "You should've cleared that easy."

Dareth hung his head and said nothing.

One of the boys he knew in the Eagles team patted him on the back as he ran back to the centre circle.

"Cheers, Dareth," he laughed.

The goal gave Kyle's dad the opportunity he'd been waiting for.

"What's the matter with you, Kyle? Can't you hold onto anything?" he jeered.

Mr Davies turned to his keeper with baited breath. How would he react, he wondered?

Kyle glared across at his dad. But he didn't say anything. He just picked up the ball and booted it towards the halfway line. Then he walked back to his goal.

There was barely time for Bad Boyz to kick off before the referee's whistle blew for half-time. The game was in the balance at 1–1.

10

While Bad Boyz devoured their Jaffa Cakes, Mr Davies took Dareth aside.

"What's the matter, Dareth?" he asked.

"Nuffing," Dareth shrugged.

"Come on, Dareth. There must be something wrong."

"Everyone has an off-day sometimes," said Dareth defensively. "David Beckham don't play well all the time, does he?"

"I know," said Mr Davies. "But, well, you're playing pants." He thought this might make Dareth smile. But it didn't. He just shrugged again.

"I'm doin' me best," he said simply. Mr Davies just had to hope that his best would be a lot better in the second half.

It wasn't.

If Dareth was pants in the first half, he was great big granny knickers in the second. His control was bad, his shooting was terrible and he kept on giving the ball away.

Eddy's Eagles definitely had the upper hand. The equalizer had boosted their confidence and they seized on Dareth's mistakes to mount several dangerous attacks. Fortunately, Kyle's nerve was still holding in the face of some cruel taunts from the touch-line. He made a string of fine saves. In front of him, Sadiq, Max and Jordan were brilliant. They chased and harried and tackled as if their lives depended on it. Time after time, they kept the Eagles at bay. But the pressure was growing and they were getting tired.

When the breakthrough came, though, it was entirely self-inflicted – and once again, Dareth was the culprit. As with the equalizer, the Eagles' second goal came from a corner. The ball was crossed to the near post, where Dareth was standing. The ball was moving quite slowly and it should have been a simple task for the Bad Boyz skipper to kick it clear. But he didn't. Instead, he took a step back into the goal mouth and, with a gentle flick of his boot, helped the ball into the net.

There were yelps of delight from the Eagles players. But everywhere else the goal was met with stunned silence. The Bad Boyz players stood staring at Dareth, dumbfounded, totally speechless, as if they could not believe what they had just seen. On the touch-line, the spectators of both sides were equally shocked – and none more so than Mr Davies. Own goals happened. They were no one's fault, usually, just bad luck. But this own goal was very much someone's fault. Dareth, it appeared, had quite deliberately deflected the ball into his own goal. But why would he want to do that? It didn't make sense.

It was such a bizarre act that no one seemed to know how to react to it. Normally Bad Boyz were quick to blame if blame was due, but today they said nothing.

The match continued in a strangely muted atmosphere. Even Kyle's dad was quiet. It seemed that the final would peter out tamely and Eddy's Eagles would take the cup.

But the drama wasn't over yet.

With barely a minute remaining, a lucky bounce put one of the Eagles players through on goal with only Kyle to beat. The keeper hesitated, unsure whether to advance or stay his ground. His dad was in no doubt.

"Move yourself, Kyle, you great lump. You're too slow to catch a snail."

For an instant, Kyle's attention was distracted as he flashed a scowl across at his dad. And it was at that instant that the Eagles forward shot. He hit the ball hard and true, a magnificent strike curving towards the corner of the goal.

But it never got there.

Flinging himself backwards and sideways with more agility than anyone expected, Kyle reached the ball and clung onto it with both hands.

Applause greeted his effort from all around the touch-line.

"Great save, Kyle!" Mr Davies called.

But Kyle wasn't finished. He ran to the edge of his area, and with a quick glance up he kicked the ball deep into the Eagles half. It was an enormous kick and just what Sung-Woo had been waiting for. In a second, he was on to the ball; in another, he'd lifted an exquisite left-footed half-volley over the helpless Eagles keeper and into the net. At the last gasp, Bad Boyz had equalized!

As the outfield players mobbed a smiling Sung-Woo, Kyle turned to the touch-line and raised a triumphant fist to Mr Davies and then, with a beam of grinning satisfaction, to his dad.

Moments later, the final whistle went. The result was a draw. The two teams would have to replay the final the following week.

11 ⚽

The Bad Boyz dressing-room was wild with joy. To save a match they'd come so close to losing had sent the team's spirits soaring. Max and Bloomer danced about with their shirts over their heads; Sadiq and Jordan went through a complicated ritual of slapping hands; Kyle sat with a wall-to-wall smile. Even Sung-Woo was happy – he was humming tunelessly to himself. Only Dareth was out of step with the mood. He sat on his own in a corner of the changing-room, looking bleak.

No one spoke to him either in anger or in celebration and he said nothing either. He got changed quickly and sidled away.

Mr Davies caught him at the door. "Come outside, Dareth," he said. "I want a word."

It was no good, though: Mr Davies could get

nothing out of his skipper. The goal had been an accident, he said. He hadn't meant to do it. It had just been a mistake. He repeated what he'd said at half-time about having an off-day.

As they were talking, the two boys that Dareth knew on the Eagles side appeared. In full view of the Bad Boyz coach, one of them raised a finger at Dareth and then, very deliberately, drew it across his throat, as if threatening dire consequences.

There was definitely something going on, Mr Davies was sure of that. And if Bad Boyz were going to have a chance of winning the cup, then he needed to find out just what it was.

On Monday, at school, Mr Davies tried again. He got Dareth to stay behind in the classroom when everyone else went off for lunch. This time his tack was more direct.

"Is there something going on with you and those Eagles boys?" he asked. "Have you made some sort of deal with them?"

Dareth shook his head.

"Dareth, don't lie to me," Mr Davies said. "That was no off-day you were having on

Saturday. You were doing your best to make us lose."

"No, I never, I..."

"Yes?"

Dareth shrugged.

"I know you're no angel, Dareth, but I never figured you for a cheat – or a traitor."

It was melodramatic, but it worked. Dareth's eyes flashed with indignation.

"I ain't a cheat or a traitor!" he yelped. His face creased in misery. "They made me do it, didn't they!"

"Who? Those boys?"

"Dexter and Ashley, yeah."

"How could they make you? Did they threaten you with violence?" Mr Davies probed.

"Nah, I could do them any day," Dareth snorted. "They got somefing on me, ain't they."

"What?"

Dareth sighed. "Well, you know I said their dad's got a shop? Well, now and then I used to nick things, didn't I. Nuffing big, just biscuits and drinks and stuff like that."

"You shoplifted?"

"Yeah. Sometimes. Dexter and Ash did an' all."

"Well, that's different, isn't it? They're his sons."

"Yeah, well so was I, practically. Brian – that's his dad – was always round our place, making himself at home, helping himself to our food and stuff. I reckoned he owed us somefing, the tight-arse."

Mr Davies pursed his lips thoughtfully. "But I still don't see what these boys have got on you," he said.

"The shop's got one of them cameras," Dareth answered. "They got me on film."

"And they're threatening to show it to their dad if you don't help them win the cup?"

"Yeah. And Brian'll go to the police, I know he will. He 'ates me, since Mum gave him the elbow. Then they'll find out about Mum and that I'm livin' with me gran and then..."

"You're worried that Social Services will take you into care, I know." They'd been through all this before. Mr Davies gave his captain a searching look.

"Well, Dareth, what are you going to do about it?" he asked.

Dareth shrugged once more. "I dunno. What can I do?"

"You can try talking to Brian. Apologize. Offer to pay him back for what you stole," Mr Davies suggested. "You'll have to do something, Dareth. I can't allow you to play on Saturday if this isn't resolved. It wouldn't be fair on the others. To be frank, with you playing like you did on Saturday, they'd be better off without you."

Dareth looked horrified. "You can't leave me out!"

"Yeah, I can, Dareth. And I will. So you'd better think about how you're going to solve this problem. And fast."

12 ⚽

The following days were the most worrying yet for the Bad Boyz coach. How would Dareth react? Would he make an effort to sort out his problem? And if he didn't, could Mr Davies really leave him out of the team? What would the others say?

The day before the Cup Final replay, Mr Davies called his team together at lunchtime for a meeting in his classroom.

"Aren't we going out on the field to practise?" Bloomer questioned.

"Not today, Bloomer," said Mr Davies grimly. "There are things we need to sort out."

"I got this new trick I wanted to show you," said Bloomer disappointedly.

"Well, save it for the match tomorrow," Mr Davies told him. "You can surprise us."

"Yeah," Jordan agreed, "you can do something sensible. That'd be a mega surprise."

When lunchtime came and the Bad Boyz team assembled, there was one notable absentee.

"Where's Dareth?" Mr Davies asked.

"He ain't here," said Kyle.

"Yes, I can see that, Kyle. But where is he?"

"He went home," said Max. "He said he had to do something."

At that instant, the door opened and in walked Dareth. His face wore a broad grin.

"Sorry I'm late," he said. "I had an appointment."

"What sort of appointment?" Mr Davies asked.

"Down Brian's shop. I went to talk to him – like you said I should."

Mr Davies shook his head. "I didn't say you should go during school-time, Dareth. That's against school rules, you know it is."

Dareth shrugged. He wasn't very good at keeping the school rules. "Oh, right, sorry," he said. Then he smiled once more. "Anyway, I got it sorted," he added cheerfully. The others all looked at him blankly. They knew something had been up, but they didn't know what.

"I think you'd better explain," Mr Davies said.

Briefly Dareth explained his problem and how he'd solved it. He'd finally plucked up the courage to go to talk to the shopkeeper. He was going to tell him about the blackmail his sons were doing, hoping that he'd be madder with them for that crime than he would with Dareth for the shoplifting. He wasn't very hopeful, but, as Mr Davies had said, he had to do something. When he got to the shop, though, Brian wasn't there. Nor were his sons. Alfie, the shop assistant, was in charge. He and Dareth got on OK. Dareth told him his problem. Alfie shook his head and laughed. He told Dareth not to worry. The camera was just for watching people in the shop, he said, it didn't have film in it. Brian was too mean to buy any.

"So Dexter and Ash was having me on," Dareth concluded. "They never had no tape."

"Good," said Mr Davies. He gave Dareth a tough look. "But you shouldn't have taken the stuff in the first place, should you?"

"Nah, I s'pose not," Dareth agreed.

"And you're not going to do it again, are you?"

"Nah," said Dareth quickly.

Max tutted loudly. "You're a bad boy, Dareth," he scolded. Then he smiled. "You didn't nick us any biscuits or anything when you were in the shop, did you?" he asked hopefully.

"Max!" growled Mr Davies.

"Sorry," said Max. He pulled a long face and hung his head as if in shame. The others laughed – except Sadiq, who was scowling.

"I reckon we should get those Eagles cheats," he said.

"Yeah," Kyle agreed.

"So you will," said Mr Davies. "By going out there tomorrow and winning."

The cheer that greeted this statement suggested that Bad Boyz intended to do just that.

13 ⚽

There was further good news for Bad Boyz on the morning of the final. Kyle's dad had gone. He'd got in some trouble the night before and, when the police had been called, he'd run away. The word was that he'd left town to avoid getting arrested.

"I don't care what he does no more, anyway," said Kyle. "I wouldn't care if he was here."

"I'm glad he's not, though," said Jordan, and Kyle agreed.

Mr Davies was pleased to see that they had a couple more supporters this week. Mr Machin, chairman of Doorstop Dairies, the Bad Boyz sponsors, had come along to watch – and so had Sung-Woo's older brother. Sung-Woo pointed him out when Bad Boyz ran onto the pitch. Not that there was any doubt about whose relative he was. He wore an almost identical pair of glasses to Sung-Woo and had the same serious expression.

When Dareth went forward to the centre circle for the toss-up, Dexter and Ash made sure he had to go past them. They shook their fingers at him and made a few threatening remarks under their breath as he walked by. Dareth showed no emotion, but inside he was smiling: they thought they had him in their pockets. Well, they were going to get a big shock.

Their first surprise came straight from the kick-off. Ash took it and passed to Dexter. Wham! Dareth was on the Eagles player in a flash and off with the ball. Dexter didn't know what had hit him. The Bad Boyz players were a bit surprised too. They didn't get forward quickly enough to support Dareth and his run came to nothing. His sharpness soon had an effect on the rest of the team, though.

After the blip of the week before, they were back to their best. The passing was crisp, the movement swift and the tackling tigerish. The Eagles were simply swept aside. With a lot of luck and some desperate defending, they managed to hold out until midway through the first half, but then Sung-Woo scored with a brilliant volley and Bad Boyz were really on their way. Soon after, Sadiq headed a second from a corner and then Dareth jinked past three defenders and smashed a shot high in the net to put Bad Boyz three up at half-time.

The second half was more of the same. Bad Boyz swarmed forward – even Max and Sadiq took it in turns to join in the attacks. Behind them, Kyle had little to do, though he did foil Ash with a fair but bone-shuddering challenge when the Eagles forward was clean through on goal. Picking himself up, the big keeper turned to Dareth with a massive grin and a thumbs-up. Ash, meanwhile, rolled around on the ground, moaning. He soon got up, though, when his manager ran on and poured cold water over him.

While this was going on, Dexter and Dareth were standing almost together on the halfway line. "We're gonna get you," the Eagles player whispered fiercely.

Dareth smiled. "What you goin' to do? Tell your old man?"

"Yeah," said Dexter. "When we show him that tape, you're going to be dogmeat."

Dareth's smile broadened. "There ain't no tape," he said. "And you can tell your old man from me that he's a stingy tight-arse and I'm glad me mum gave him the elbow."

Dexter was fuming. He followed Dareth around, trying to foul him. But with Dareth in the form he was, it was almost impossible for the Eagles player to catch him. He was quite outstanding – Dr Jekyll to last week's Mr Hyde. He set up a goal for Jordan and another for Sung-Woo.

The sixth and final goal, though, was all of Bloomer's making – and his trickery surprised everyone. When he got the ball out on the left of the penalty area, there didn't seem to be much on. But suddenly he hooked the ball up against his standing leg, juggled it and then lifted it over the defender's head, straight into Dareth's path.

Dareth could have shot straight away, but instead stepped inside a tackle to get the ball on his right foot. As he did so, Dexter, seeing the opportunity finally to catch his enemy, slid in with both feet and clogged him. Dareth went down hard, but, fortunately, he wasn't hurt. The referee pointed to the penalty spot, then gave Dexter a stern talking-to.

Dareth placed the ball on the spot. There was never a moment's doubt in his head that he was going to score. This was his moment of triumph – and revenge for the humiliation of the previous week. When the whistle blew, he strode forward and blasted the ball into the top right-hand corner of the net. Then he turned towards Ash and Dexter, cupped one hand round his ear and began to flap the other in his familiar celebration.

Minutes later, applauded by the spectators from both sides, Bad Boyz stepped forward, one by one, to receive their medals from Stan Reynolds: Kyle, Jordan, Bloomer, Sadiq, Max, Sung-Woo and, finally, Dareth.

"That was a bit better than last week, son, wasn't it?" the league secretary remarked as he handed Dareth his medal.

"Yeah," Dareth agreed. Then he held out his hands to take the cup. The next moment he was waving the silver trophy in the air with jubilation.

Bad Boyz were the knock-out kings!

Follow Bad Boyz on tour in France in the fourth
book of this series:

BARMY ARMY

(Turn the page to read the first chapter.)

1

"*Bonjour, mes choux! J'ai des bonnes nouvelles. Nous allons jouer au football en France!*"

Mr Davies beamed out at the seven children sitting in front of him in the classroom. Together, they made up the little league football team Bad Boyz. As well as being the children's teacher at school, Mr Davies was the Bad Boyz manager. At this moment, his team were all gaping back at him as if he'd just grown purple fins.

"Eh?" grunted Kyle, the Bad Boyz keeper, at last.

"Are you all right, sir?" enquired Dareth, the team's skipper. "Would yer like some water or sumfing?"

Mr Davies shook his head. "I was

speaking French," he explained.

"Oh yeah, *bonjour*," Jordan nodded. "I know that. I saw it tagged on a wall in town somewhere." Jordan was very keen on graffiti. Her tagging exploits had got her into a lot of trouble in the past.

"It means 'good day'," said Mr Davies: "hello."

"'ello," Dareth responded with a broad grin.

Mr Davies ignored him. "I was telling you that I had some good news," he went on. "We're going to play football in France."

"In France?" squeaked Bloomer, his cheeks flaring pink. "That's ... well ... it's ... not in this country, is it?"

"Duh, well done, Bloomer!" Jordan scoffed. "Of course it's not in this country. It's a completely *different* country."

"We're going to France, we're going to France!" exclaimed Max dramatically, and he banged his head down on the desk in a pretend faint.

Sung-Woo put up his hand.

"Yes, Sung-Woo?" said Mr Davies.

Sung-Woo frowned. "I no understand," he

muttered seriously, "why you say hello to your shoe."

"Yeah, you did, sir," piped Bloomer. "You said 'bonjewer my shoe'."

"*Bonjour,* mes choux," Mr Davies corrected him. "It's a term of endearment the French use. It means 'Hello, my cabbages'."

"Eh? You what?" Kyle uttered. "We ain't cabbages."

"No," agreed Bloomer shrilly, "we're not vegetables."

"*We* aren't," said Jordan, "*you* are."

"No, we all are," said Max surprisingly.

"What d'yer mean?" Kyle demanded. His podgy face crinkled like a deflating beach ball.

"Well, we're human *beans*. Get it?" Max declared. He rolled his eyes and stuck out his tongue.

Everyone laughed except Sung-Woo, who looked more confused than ever.

"It was a joke, Sung-Woo," said Mr Davies. He raised his eyebrows at Max. "And not a very good one. Now let's get back to the subject... The Appleton Little League has a link with a similar league in France. They've invited us, as Little League champions, to go to France to play two matches against the winners of their league. A sort of continental championship, I suppose. What do you say to that?" His gaze fell on Sadiq. "Sadiq, you've been very quiet," he said. "What do you think?"

Sadiq was rarely slow in voicing his opinion to teachers – or anyone else, come to that. It had often got him into detention. Today, though, he had been unusually silent.

"Yeah, it sounds all right," he said without enthusiasm.

"All right?" queried Mr Davies. "Is that the best you can do?"

Sadiq shrugged. "It sounds good," he ventured, but still without real enthusiasm.

"It sounds wicked," Dareth asserted. "I've never been to France."

"Have any of you ever been abroad?" Mr Davies asked. "Apart from Sung-Woo." Sung-Woo had lived abroad until less than a year ago.

"I been to Spain," said Jordan.

"Me too," squawked Bloomer.

"I been to Greece," said Max. "Grease

74

Lightning," he sang, and started to jig around in a weird kind of dance.

Mr Davies raised his eyes again. "Anyone else?" he prompted.

Dareth put up his hand. "I've been to Iceland," he said. He ran his hand over his cropped head and grinned. "Me gran gets her frozen sausages there."

Mr Davies shook his head and sighed.

Author's Note

Although Appleton Little League is my own creation, it's based on an organization that really exists. Little League Football is a registered charity that provides free football for children from eight to thirteen years old in over thirty leagues around the country. The emphasis is on enthusiasm and effort rather than ability – players are encouraged to develop team spirit, self-discipline and sportsmanship. It's also a lot of fun and a good place to start playing organized football. Players join individually rather than as a team, as in my series, but most of the rules are as I've described them. If you want to find out more, check out the Little League Football website:

www.littleleaguefootball.com

There may be a league on your doorstep!

If you're interested in joining a Sunday junior football team, a useful site to look at is:

www.juniorleague.net

It has details of teams and leagues right across the country.

If you like playing football, there's a team out there for you!

To ask Alan Durant anything about the Bad Boyz series – or any football matter – you can contact him by e-mail at:

alan.durant@walker.co.uk

He'd love to hear from you!